For Marcia, friend of bears

LADYBIRD BOOKS, INC.
Auburn, Maine 04210 U.S.A.
© LADYBIRD BOOKS LTD 1989
Loughborough, Leicestershire, England

Printed in England

Birthday Bear

By Margo Finch
Illustrated by Kristine Bollinger

Ladybird Books

Barney was Danny's teddy bear. He went with Danny almost everywhere and slept on Danny's pillow at night. They loved each other very much.

One morning, Danny tied a red ribbon around Barney's neck. *Is today a special day?* Barney wondered. Then Danny told him, "It's my birthday, Barney! I'm four years old!"

Barney was sure that meant today would be exciting and important. He felt very festive in his fine new bow.

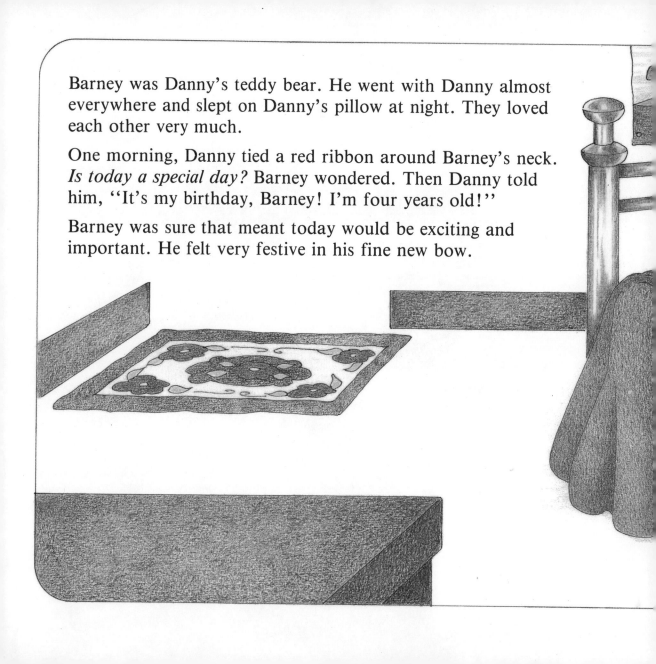

Danny and Barney went downstairs to breakfast. By Danny's chair was another surprise—a shiny red tricycle. "For our big boy," said Daddy.

And for his bear, too! Barney thought hopefully. Barney had never been on a tricycle, and he could hardly wait to have a ride.

After Danny finished eating, he and Barney
rode to the corner and back, ding-dinging the
bell all the way. "Whee!" Barney cried to
himself as the wind rushed past his ears. He
wanted to keep riding, but Danny stopped in
front of the house. Grandma and Grandpa
were coming up the walk.

"My, how big you're getting!" Grandma said to Danny. She hugged and kissed him and gave him a present—a book about dinosaurs.

Grandpa shook Barney's paw politely and said, "Well, you're a fine bear. How do you do?"

Barney thought that was a nice thing to say. He hoped Grandpa could see that he did very well, thank you.

Danny showed Barney all the pictures in his new book. Barney wished they were pictures of bears, but Danny told him such amazing things about the dinosaurs that Barney began to be quite interested. He was sorry when Danny turned the last page.

In the afternoon four of Danny's friends came to his birthday
party. There were balloons and party hats for everyone.
Danny's hat was a gold crown, and he put one just like it on
Barney's head. *Oh, my,* Barney thought, *a crown* and *a bow!*
Why couldn't every day be a birthday?

Mama brought in the birthday cake, and they all sang
"Happy birthday to you."

"Help me blow out the candles, Barney!" said Danny.
Barney did his best, and he and Danny blew out every one.
Barney even had his own serving of cake and ice cream,
which Danny kindly ate for him. "This is a wonderful party!"
Barney told himself happily.

Barney was glad when bedtime came. It had been a busy day, and he was ready to snuggle up on Danny's pillow. But Danny left Barney on the window seat and got into bed by himself.

Could Danny have forgotten me? Barney wondered. He waited for Danny to come get him, but Danny never did.

He did forget me, Barney thought. He was beginning to feel scared and lonely.

Then Mama came in. "Don't you want Barney?" she asked.

"No, thank you," said Danny.

Barney couldn't believe his ears.

"I'm a big boy now," Danny went on. "Big boys don't take their teddy bears to bed."

"Poor old Barney," said Mama. "He'll miss you."

Barney felt awful. Would he really have to sit alone on the window seat every night from now on?

Then Barney heard Danny say, "Mama, is Barney four, like me?"

"No," answered Mama. "You got him for your third birthday, so he's just one year old today."

Danny said, "Oh... then Barney's still little. Maybe I'd better have him with me then, so he won't be scared."

Suddenly Barney felt himself being lifted across the room and into Danny's arms.

Barney felt just fine now. He was back where he belonged.
Mama tucked them both in and kissed Danny good night.

"Kiss Barney too, please," said Danny. "It's his birthday too, you know."

Barney lay there on the pillow, feeling safe and happy all the way to his furry toes. The day really had turned out to be exciting and important. "It's my birthday too, you know," he said to himself. He hummed in the darkness—very quietly, so he wouldn't wake Danny—"Happy birthday to me. Happy birthday to me!"